Max
and
Zoe

The Lunchroom Fight

by Shelley Swanson Sateren

illustrated by Mary Sullivan

PICTURE WINDOW BOOKS
a capstone imprint

Max and Zoe is published by Picture Window Books,
A Capstone Imprint
1710 Roe Crest Drive
North Mankato, Minnesota 56003
www.capstonepub.com

Library of Congress Cataloging-in-Publication Data
Sateren, Shelley Swanson.
 Max and Zoe : the lunchroom fight / by Shelley Swanson Sateren ;
illustrated by Mary Sullivan.
     p. cm. -- (Max and Zoe)
 Summary: After Max and Zoe quarrel over who will sit with Anna at
the peanut-free table, they look for a solution that will make everybody
happy.
 ISBN 978-1-4048-7199-1 (library binding)
 ISBN 978-1-4795-2328-3 (paperback)
1. School lunchrooms, cafeterias, etc.--Juvenile fiction. 2. Elementary
schools--Juvenile fiction. 3. Food allergy--Juvenile fiction. 4. Best
friends--Juvenile fiction. 5. Quarreling--Juvenile fiction. [1. Cafeterias-
-Fiction. 2. Elementary schools--Fiction. 3. Schools--Fiction. 4. Food
allergy--Fiction. 5. Best friends--Fiction. 6. Friendship--Fiction.
7. Quarreling--Fiction.] I. Sullivan, Mary, 1958- ill. II. Title. III. Title:
Lunchroom fight. IV. Series: Sateren, Shelley Swanson. Max and Zoe.
PZ7.S249155Mdl 2013
 813.54--dc23
                                                    2012047380

Designer: Kristi Carlson

Printed in the United States of America in
North Mankato Minnesota.
072019   000093

Table of Contents

Just before the bell rang, Max

saw Zoe whisper to Anna. Max

knew Zoe was up to something.

Anna was allergic to peanuts.

She always sat at the lunchroom's

peanut-safe table.

Each day, Anna could pick one friend to eat with her. And every day, she had a hard time picking just one friend.

"Hey, Anna," Max said.

"Remember, pick me today!"

Anna looked at Max. Then she looked at Zoe.

"It's my turn today, Anna," he said. "You gave me your peanut promise!"

Anna took a deep breath. "I did promise," she said.

"Yes! My lucky day!" said Max.

When Max turned around, Zoe whispered to Anna again. Then she smiled.

Zoe felt a little bad, but Max would get over it. She was sure Anna would rather sit by her anyway.

At lunchtime, Max, Anna, and two other kids sat at the peanut-safe table together.

"This is so cool," Max said as he opened his lunchbox.

The peanut-safe table was in the back corner of the cafeteria. It was just at the edge of the other tables. A sign hung above it on the wall.

THIS IS A

PEANUT FREE TABLE

Max was just starting to eat when Zoe sat down.

"Um, Max?" Zoe said. "Please leave. Anna picked me today."

"No, she picked me," said Max.

Zoe looked at Anna and asked,
"You did?"

Anna said, "Uh, well . . ."

"See, Max?" said Zoe. "Go away."

"No!" Max argued and frowned.
"You go away! I am already sitting
here with Anna."

A teacher hurried over.

"Not again, Anna," she said.

"Just one friend, remember?"

Anna looked sad.

"I know," said Anna. "But I don't
want to hurt anyone's feelings!"

Max and Zoe started to argue louder.

"It's my turn!" Max said.

"No, it's mine!" yelled Zoe.

"Enough!" said the teacher.

"You will both have to move. Sorry,
Anna."

"Sorry, Anna," said Max.

"Me, too," said Zoe.

"This stinks," said Zoe.

"No kidding," said Max.

"I bet it stinks even worse for Anna," said Max. "She can't ever share snacks or eat peanut butter."

"She can't even touch a peanut! If she does, she gets sick," said Zoe.

"And now she doesn't have a friend to eat with," said Max.

He looked at Anna. She looked very sad.

Chapter 3
The Peanut Project

Max and Zoe sat quietly. They

didn't feel hungry. They just felt sad.

"Hey! I know how to help Anna,"

Max said.

He told his idea to Zoe.

"Good idea, Max," she said.

"And I'm sorry I started this mess."

"It's okay, Zoe," said Max.

"Friends fight sometimes. Now let's

get to work!"

Instead of going out for recess,

Max and Zoe asked to stay in. They

had a special project to work on.

They cut a giant peanut out of paper. They colored it and taped it on their classroom wall.

"Look, Anna!" said Max. "Now kids who want to eat with you can take turns."

"Yeah," said Zoe. "No more fights."

"Cool!" said Anna. "It's great, you guys. I'm NUT kidding!"

Max and Zoe laughed.

"We're sorry you had to eat alone today," Max said.

"It's okay," said Anna. "The sign-up sheet is an awesome idea."

By the end of the day, the entire sheet was filled with names. And the next day, everyone had a happy lunch.

About the Author

Shelley Swanson Sateren is the award-winning author of many children's books. She has worked as a children's book editor and in a children's bookstore. Today, besides writing, Shelley works with elementary-school-aged children in various settings. She lives in St. Paul, Minnesota, with her husband and two sons.

About the Illustrator

Mary Sullivan has been drawing and writing her whole life, which has mostly been spent in Texas. She earned her BFA from the University of Texas in Studio Art, but she considers herself a self-trained illustrator. Mary lives in Cedar Park, a suburb of Austin, Texas.

Glossary

allergic (uh-LUR-jik) — to have an unpleasant reaction to something, such as food and dust

argue (AR-gyoo) — to disagree with someone forcefully

cafeteria (kaf-uh-TIHR-ee-uh) — the place where students eat in school

promise (PROM-iss) — give your word that you will do something

recess (REE-sess) — a break from work

separate (SEP-uh-rate) — set apart from others

Discussion Questions

1. Anna has trouble saying no to people. Talk about a time when you felt the same way.

2. What do you think Zoe was whispering to Anna at the beginning of the story? How do you think what she said made Max feel?

3. What did you think of Max's solution to the problem? What would you have done if you were Max?

Writing Prompts

1. In the story, Max and Zoe argue. Have you ever argued with a friend? Write a sentence about it.

2. It's important to stay safe when you are in the lunchroom. Make a list of three lunchroom rules.

3. Max and Zoe become better friends to Anna. Write a few sentences about how you can become a better friend to someone.

Make Your Own Poster

You can help keep allergic kids safe. Make a sign for the peanut-safe table at your school.

What you need:

- pencil

- 1 sheet of lined paper

- 1 large sheet of brown poster paper

- scissors

- brown marker

- other color markers

- masking tape

What you do:

1. On the lined paper, make a list of peanut-safe rules. Your list might say: wash hands before sitting here; no sharing food; no tree nuts, peanuts, or peanut oil; and so on.

2. Show an adult your list. Make any changes they suggest.

3. Draw a large peanut on the poster paper.

4. Cut it out and color the outside edge brown.

5. At the top of the peanut, write PEANUT-SAFE TABLE RULES. Below the heading, write the list of rules with markers. Use different colors and draw pictures.

6. Ask the lunchroom workers or a teacher where to hang the poster.

The Fun Doesn't Stop Here!

Discover more at www.capstonekids.com

- Videos & Contests
- Games & Puzzles
- Friends & Favorites
- Authors & Illustrators